The Adventures of Goliath

Goliath and the Buried Treasure

The Adventures of Goliath

Goliath and the Buried Treasure

Terrance Dicks
Illustrated by
Valerie Littlewood

SCHOLASTIC INC.
New York Toronto London Auckland Sydney

ISBN 0-590-48912-7

12 11 10 9 8 7 6 5 4 3 2   5 6 7 8 9/9

Printed in the U.S.A.   40

First Scholastic printing, August 1994

CONTENTS

The Adventures of Goliath

Goliath and the
Buried Treasure

Chapter One

The Dog Who Loved To Dig

"No!" shouted David. "Bad dog! Stop it at once!" He was leaning out of the kitchen window, yelling at his dog Goliath in the garden below.

Goliath looked up, gave him a doggy grin, and went on with what he was doing—which happened to be digging an enormous hole in the center of David's dad's best flower bed.

David's dad looked up from his

newspaper. "Now what's that dog up to?"

He came to join David at the window.

The apartment where David lived with his mom and dad and his great big dog Goliath only had a very small garden. And it wasn't really their garden at all. It belonged to Mrs. Richards, the landlady, who lived in the upper part of the house. As she wasn't interested in gardening, she'd told David's dad he could use the

garden if he looked after it.

It wasn't much of a garden, just one patch of lawn and one flower bed, but David's dad was very proud of it.

He'd mowed and trimmed the little lawn, dug up the flower bed, and planted seeds.

Now he was waiting anxiously for something to come up.

When he looked out of the window and saw Goliath in the middle of the flower bed, digging furiously, David's dad gave a bellow of rage.

The soft earth was flying through the air, and the whole center of the flower bed was just one enormous hole.

David's dad dashed out into the garden. Seconds later he was back, chasing Goliath, who shot through the apartment like a hairy hurricane, raced up the stairs, and dived under David's bed, his usual refuge in times of danger.

4

"Come out, you great monster," yelled David's dad.

"Leave him alone, Dad," pleaded David. "He knows he's done something wrong. He won't do it again. Hadn't we better get the hole filled in before Mrs. Richards sees it?"

This cunning appeal to common sense did the trick.

Grabbing shovels from the corner of the yard, David and his dad set to work filling in the hole.

They were just patting down the earth when Mrs. Richards called out from an upstairs window, "You two are hard at work."

David's dad looked up. "Er, yes. Got to keep the soil turned over, you know, very important at this time of year."

"When am I going to see some nice flowers then?"

"Ah, that all depends," said David's dad vaguely. "We're doing our best!"

Mrs. Richards popped back inside.

David said, "Thanks, Dad."

His father smiled. "I'll forget about it—this time. But see it doesn't happen again!"

Chapter Two

Goliath's New Game

As he helped his father finish restoring the flower bed, David thought to himself that being a dog owner certainly had its problems.

Owning a dog like Goliath gave you *big* problems.

That was the thing about Goliath, he was big. Really big.

Not that he'd started out that way.

Goliath had been just another mongrel puppy, the smallest and weakest of the litter, what dog breeders call the runt. David had chosen him because he felt sorry for him.

Thanks to David's loving care, Goliath had grown strong and healthy—and he had grown and grown and grown.

Now he was the biggest dog for miles around, a mixture of a German shepherd, wolfhound, and mastiff, with a bit of Old English sheepdog thrown in.

Goliath was a fine-looking dog all right, but he wasn't quite as impressive as he looked. For all his huge size, he was really rather timid and not all that bright. He could be very obstinate as well. When Goliath got an idea into his head, it was hard to shift.

Digging holes was Goliath's latest craze.

It had all started during one of their walks on the local Common. The Common was a big area of open ground, with grass and woods, trees and ponds. Unlike the local park, it was still fairly wild—a bit of real country in the center of town.

They had just met Miss Hollings, David's history teacher, and her Yorkshire terrier, Scrap.

Despite the difference in their sizes, Scrap and Goliath were great friends, and they both rushed off to play, while David stayed chatting with Miss Hollings. She was one of David's favorite teachers, tall and thin and rather vague. She always seemed to be concerned for some good cause, whales or elephants or seals, or worrying about chemical

waste or aerosol sprays.

This week it was the Common.

"It's really disgraceful, David," she said. "All these years we thought the Common was protected. Now some property speculator has found a loophole in the regulations and wants to build apartments on it."

David nodded. This was a worry David could share. Like most local children, he spent a lot of time on the Common.

Where could he take Goliath for his walks, if the Common disappeared? There was the local park of course, but that was far too small and too formal for a big clumsy dog like Goliath.

There were flower beds in the park, jealously guarded by fierce park keepers, and the grass was the kind you had to keep off. It would never do for Goliath.

"Can't you find some way to stop them building?" asked David.

"Well, we did have hopes about Boadicea's Mound."

Boadicea's Mound was a big hump in the middle of the Common. It was named for the famous warrior queen who had led the Britons against the Romans. Some people even believed that she was buried in the Mound.

"It's never been properly investigated, you know, and the local Archaeological Society is trying to get it declared a site of historical interest. That might be the answer . . ."

Miss Hollings rattled on, and suddenly David noticed a big disturbance in the bushes and saw a little fountain of earth flying through the air.

He pointed. "What's going on?"

"Oh, that's Scrap's latest craze," said Miss Hollings. "Digging!"

"What started him off?" asked David.

"I gave him a bone, and he dug a hole and buried it in the garden. Then he forgot where it was and started digging holes everywhere.

Now he can't seem to stop digging wherever we go."

David went over to have a look.

Sure enough, just behind the bush, Scrap was digging furiously, earth flying up behind him.

Goliath sat looking on, head cocked, a rather puzzled expression on his face.

When David came up, Scrap
stopped digging, deciding, it
seemed, that his missing bone
wasn't here after all. He trotted
back to Miss Hollings.

Goliath sat looking thoughtfully
at the hole.

Suddenly he started digging
furiously, scrabbling away with his
enormous feet.

This time the earth really started
flying.

The hole grew bigger and bigger
and bigger. Obviously, Goliath had
a gift for digging.

He scrabbled away, enlarging the
hole all the time, until it grew so big
David started getting worried.

Although the Common wasn't a
public park, there *were* park keepers
of a sort, men in green suits and

odd-shaped hats.

David knew there were rules against lighting fires and playing radios. For all he knew, there were rules against digging great holes as well.

"No, Goliath," he yelled. "That's enough. Stop it!"

Full of enthusiasm for his new game, Goliath chose not to hear. Grabbing the big dog by his collar, David put Goliath's leash on and hauled him away.

Goliath came reluctantly, looking over his shoulder at his precious hole.

David had quite a fight to get him home.

After the disaster in the garden, David did his best to cure Goliath of his craze for digging.

As soon as the work was finished, David lured Goliath out from under the bed and led him out into the garden, pointing at the filled-in hole. "No, Goliath," he said sternly. "Bad dog! No. No digging!"

Goliath hung his head and whimpered pathetically. He hated being told off.

David took him back inside, convinced there would be no more digging in his dad's flower bed.

And he was quite right.

What happened next was worse. Much worse!

Chapter Three

Goliath Goes Wild

It happened a few days later.

David was sitting with his mom and dad, discussing Goliath's behavior.

"He really is sorry, Dad," said David. "He's been good as gold ever since."

David's dad lowered his paper. "I should hope so! I had to replant that entire flower bed. Heaven knows when Mrs. Richards will see any flowers now."

"We could buy some plastic ones and stick them in," suggested David. "Bet she'd never notice the difference!"

"Where is Goliath anyway?" asked David's mom.

They looked around. No Goliath.

David's dad rushed to the window and looked out. David and his mom followed. The newly dug flower bed was perfectly smooth. No Goliath, no holes. "Well, as long as he's not digging up my flower bed," said David's dad.

Suddenly there came a shout from next door.

It was more of a yell, really.

A terrible howl of rage and despair. It came from Mr. MacGregor's garden.

Mr. MacGregor was the nice old Scotsman who lived next door.

Unlike David's dad, Mr. MacGregor was a *real* gardener. He'd worked for the Parks Department for most of his life, and now that he was retired the only garden he had to worry about was his own.

And worry about it he did.

He was always out in his garden, digging and potting and weeding and raking and doing all the other things gardeners do pretty well all day long.

As a result, Mr. MacGregor's garden put on just as fine a display of flowers as any public park.

Mr. MacGregor didn't often leave his garden. However, he must have left it for a little while this afternoon. Probably just long enough to have a cup of tea.

Just long enough for Goliath to jump over the garden fence and dig an enormous hole—right in the middle of Mr. MacGregor's best flower bed.

David and his dad arrived at the window just at the moment when Mr. MacGregor came out of his house and saw the hole.

Which accounted for that terrible cry of rage.

Mr. MacGregor was normally a kindly old gentleman.

He liked dogs in general and Goliath in particular.

He always gave Goliath a pat on the head when they met in the street.

But at the sight of the hole in his flower bed, the blood of Mr. MacGregor's Highland ancestors

began to boil.

Grabbing his shovel, he dashed toward Goliath like a wild Highland warrior brandishing his sword.

It was clear he intended to give Goliath a pat on the head of a very different kind.

Goliath liked Mr. MacGregor, too. When he saw his old friend coming toward him, he gave a bark

of welcome and wagged his tail.

But Goliath was no fool.

When he saw that his old friend was howling with rage and waving a shovel, Goliath realized something was wrong. Goliath reacted the same way he always did when there was any danger.

He turned and ran for his life.

Watched from the window by David and his dad, who were still

too horrified to move, Mr.
MacGregor chased Goliath three
times around his garden, gaining
on him all the time.

Just as he was about to catch up,
Goliath sailed over the garden fence
like a champion steeplechaser, landed
in his own garden, raced
through the open door, shot

through the kitchen, thundered up the stairs, and disappeared under David's bed.

Mr. MacGregor could run surprisingly fast for a man of his age, but he couldn't jump fences.

He glared at the fence, flung down his shovel, and turned and marched angrily into his house.

A few seconds later, there came an angry ringing at the front doorbell. David looked up at his dad. "Oh, no!"

"Oh, yes," said David's dad grimly. "Come and face the music!"

It took them *ages* to calm Mr. MacGregor down.

He threatened to go to the police.

He threatened to sue Goliath for trespass and malicious damage.

(David had a sudden picture of

Goliath in court. Goliath told off by the judge and sent to prison.)

But of course you can't take a dog to court. It's the owner who is responsible.

Goliath was David's dog, but since he was too young, it would be his poor old dad who'd be dragged before the judge.

David and his dad apologized— about ten million times! They offered to pay for any damage and to fill in the hole themselves.

Mr. MacGregor said the damage was beyond price, "All my best begonias!" He wouldn't have them setting foot in his garden.

However, since he really *was* a kindly old man, he calmed down eventually and said he'd forget all about it. Just this once.

"But ye'd best keep your great hairy beastie out 'o my garrrden," he growled, rolling his r's ferociously.

Once David's dad had calmed Mr. MacGregor down, that left David with the task of calming down his dad.

This time, David's dad said Goliath would really have to go!

"Great furry fool of a dog!" he shouted. "I'd give him away if I thought anyone would have him!"

Eventually he calmed down, too, though only after stern warnings that this must never, *never* happen again.

"I'm sure it won't, Dad," pleaded David. "Being chased like that by Mr. MacGregor must have given Goliath a terrible shock. He's learned his lesson by now!"

Just to make absolutely sure, David gave Goliath a warning of his own.

Coaxing him out of his hiding place, he led the quaking dog to the window and pointed to the next-door garden, where Mr. MacGregor was already filling in the hole and replanting with fresh flowers from his greenhouse.

"*No*, Goliath!" said David sternly.

Goliath hung his head. His tail and ears drooped.

David marched Goliath out into the garden and pointed to the spot where the first hole had been dug. "*No! No!*" said David, even more sternly.

To make absolutely sure, he even took Goliath back on the Common and found the exact spot where

Scrap had shown Goliath how to dig.

David pointed to the hole. "No, no, *no*!" he thundered. "No digging! No digging anywhere at all!"

Goliath hung his head and whimpered pathetically.

The treatment worked.

At least it seemed to work.

Goliath gave up digging holes.

Whenever he went in the garden he sat innocently by the flower bed with an angelic look on his face, as if to say, "Me? Dig holes? The very idea!"

David relaxed.

Little did he realize that Goliath would soon be digging his biggest and most spectacular hole of all— with David urging him to do it!

Chapter Four

Buried Treasure

It happened just a couple of days later. David was taking Goliath for his after-school walk on the Common when he met Miss Hollings again.

She was still worried about the Common.

Apparently plans for building were going ahead, and the builder was threatening to send in his bulldozer in a few days' time.

"What about Boadicea's Mound?" asked David.

Miss Hollings sighed. "The trouble is that the City Council is taking so much time to decide. I think quite a few of them are really on the side of the property developer. I'm going to take a party of councilors to visit the Mound tomorrow morning, on behalf of the Archaeological Society. We'll do our best to persuade them it's an important site—but we've no real evidence, you see. The only way we could *get* the evidence is by doing a proper dig, but I'm afraid they just won't give us time."

Goliath was playing with Scrap nearby. His ears pricked up at the sound of the forbidden word. He gave David a worried look and then hung his head.

David patted him. "It's all right, Goliath, we're not talking about you." David broke off, staring into space with his mouth open.

"What's the matter?" asked Miss Hollings. "Don't you feel well?"

David gulped. "I've just had an idea."

"What about?"

"Never mind," said David, politely but firmly. "I think it would be better if you didn't know anything about it. Just tell me this, what time are the councilors coming to inspect the Mound?"

"Tomorrow morning at nine o'clock."

David thought hard. He'd have to get busy right away. He grabbed Goliath by the collar, put him back on his leash, and hurried off.

"Where are you going?" called Miss Hollings.

"Back to school," called David. "Don't worry, Miss Hollings, I'll see you in the morning."

Luckily, David's school was also the local community center. It was always open after school hours, for things like exercise classes and pottery and adult education.

David hurried through the gates and tied Goliath to the school railings.

Old Mr. Roberts the caretaker popped out of his little office. "Hullo, my lad, what are you doing here? Haven't you had enough of the place, eh? Can't wait till Monday?" He laughed wheezily,

patting Goliath on the head.

"I've just got to get something for Miss Hollings," said David. "Won't be a minute. Keep an eye on Goliath for me, will you please?"

Before Mr. Roberts could answer, David had disappeared into the school. After all, he thought, he wasn't *exactly* telling lies. He really was getting something for Miss Hollings, even if she didn't know about it yet!

David paid a brief visit to his classroom and then turned to leave. On his way out he passed the school office. It was empty, with the door standing open. David paused. After all, it was all in a good cause.

He slipped inside and picked up the telephone and dialed.

A few minutes later, David was back in the playground. Goliath was just gobbling up some scraps, the remains of Mr. Roberts' snack.

"He was looking so pathetic I was sure he was hungry," explained Mr. Roberts'.

"Greedy, more like it," said David

severely. "Come on, you!"

Untying Goliath from the railings, he said good-bye to Mr. Roberts and hurried away.

"Dig! Goliath," said David urgently. "Come on, you great furry idiot, dig!"

It was next morning just before nine, and they were out on the Common. In fact, they were standing on top of Boadicea's Mound. Goliath looked up at David in puzzlement. All those scoldings, all those warnings, and now he was being *told* to dig?

Goliath couldn't believe it. He hung his head and looked confused. Was it a trap, or some kind of test?

"Dig!" hissed David. "It's all right, just this once!" But David's

treatment had worked too well. Goliath refused to move.

Frantically, David began digging himself, using the little trowel he had brought along with him.

As soon as he had the beginnings of a hole, he looked encouragingly at Goliath. "There you are. Like that. Go on, dig!"

Goliath wouldn't.

David heard a buzz of voices.

A group of serious-looking people were walking across the Common toward the Mound. In the middle of them, David recognized the tall figure of Miss Hollings. She was bringing up the councilors. There wasn't much time.

David dropped to his knees and began throwing up earth with his hands, imitating a digging dog. "Come on, Goliath, dig like this!"

It worked.

Goliath stared unbelievingly at David for a moment, and then with a woof of delight he jumped into the hole and started digging. Digging with all the pent-up enthusiasm of a dog who had been forbidden to dig for days and days.

The earth fairly flew through the air, and the hole grew and grew and grew.

By the time Miss Hollings and her councilors had reached the top of the Mound, the hole was enormous. Goliath was inside it, still digging away.

Leaving it to the last minute, David jumped into the hole and pulled Goliath out. Or rather he tried to. Goliath was well into his stride by now and didn't want to stop.

Surrounded by the astonished councilors, Miss Hollings stared down at the struggling pair in amazement. "David! What are you *doing* down there? What's going on?" With a final heave, David pulled Goliath out of the hole. "I'm awfully sorry, Miss Hollings. I was taking Goliath for a walk, and he suddenly rushed up here and started digging. I tried to stop him, but he was determined, as if he'd scented something!"

"Well, you'd better take him away," said Miss Hollings severely. "These ladies and gentlemen are from the City Council, and they've come to take a look at this site."

David held out his hand. "There's something else, Miss Hollings. When I was pulling Goliath out of the hole I found these!"

Lying on David's rather grubby palm were several irregularly shaped coins, covered with mud.

Miss Hollings took them, cleaned them, examined them closely, and then raised her voice excitedly.

"Ladies and gentlemen!
Although it is of course deplorable
that this boy's dog should dig up
the Common, by a happy accident
he has given me the proof I need."
She held out her hand. "These
coins are Roman! Most are copper,
but two at least are silver. And who
knows what a proper dig may
reveal!"

Immediately, there was a really
tremendous fuss.

People crowded around,
struggling to get a look at the
Roman coins.

Suddenly, there were a series of
very bright flashes. A press
photographer appeared and began
shooting off flashbulbs like a
machine gun. He took pictures of
David and Goliath (Goliath jumped

and tried to run from the flash when the flashbulb went off). He took pictures of Miss Hollings with the coins in her hand and the councilors crowding around.

As David slipped away, he heard a councilor saying, "But are you quite sure the coins are genuine?"

Miss Hollings said positively, "Oh yes! Roman history happens to be my specialty, and we have some coins very like these on display in our school museum."

David grinned to himself and tugged Goliath away.

Chapter Five

David's Secret

Next Monday after school, Miss Hollings told David what had happened. The photographer had been from the local paper, covering the story. The Archaeological Society had spent the whole weekend doing a proper dig on the Mound. "We didn't find Boadicea's Tomb, I'm afraid, or her treasure either. We didn't even find any more coins. But we did find clear evidence that the Mound had been the rubbish heap of some kind of Roman camp. The City Council's put a protection order on the Common, and the builder has given up!"

David laughed. "A rubbish heap? That's a bit of a disappointment, isn't it, after the Tomb of Boadicea?"

"Don't you believe it," said Miss Hollings. "You can learn a *tremendous* amount about ancient societies from their rubbish heaps. Broken pots and tools and weapons, all kinds of fascinating things . . . There may not even *be* any gold or silver, but there's treasure of another kind. The treasure of knowledge!" She frowned. "As a matter of fact, it's very odd that you found those coins

there at all—though it was lucky
that you did. I wanted to compare
them with the ones we had at
school—but those coins seem to
have disappeared."

"No, they haven't," said David. "I
borrowed them for a while—but I
gave them back to you on Saturday
morning."

Miss Hollings stared at him. "What? You mean those coins you found at the Mound . . ."

David nodded. "That's right. They were the ones from school. I took them there myself, got Goliath to dig, and then 'found' them when you all turned up. And the photographer wasn't just luck, either. I telephoned the local paper on Friday and told them there was going to be an amazing discovery on the Common on Saturday morning."

Miss Hollings gasped. "So it was all you? The hole and the coins and the photographer and everything?"

"Well, we don't want to lose the Common, do we?" said David cheerfully. "And you said yourself, the Mound really *is* a valuable archaeological site."

Miss Hollings shook her head. She seemed terribly upset.

David grinned. "Don't worry, Miss Hollings, Goliath will get all the credit. He always does!"

A few days later the story appeared in the local paper. There was a big picture of Goliath. The headline to the story read, *Dog with a Nose for Buried Treasure.* (They still hadn't found any treasure, but everyone was still hoping, and anyway, it made a nice headline.)

David and his mom and dad sat in the kitchen reading and re-reading the story.

"It's good that dog can't read," said David's dad. "He'll be getting a swelled head."

David turned to Goliath. "How does it feel to be famous?"

Goliath wasn't there.

David rushed to the window—just in time to see Goliath leaping over the fence into Mr. MacGregor's garden.

"Oh, no!" yelled David, and he rushed down to the garden. He ran to the fence. "Goliath, come back, you bad dog!"

Then he stoppped, astonished.

Mr. MacGregor was in the garden with Goliath.

And he was smiling.

In his hand was a packet of dog biscuits, and he was tossing them to Goliath, one by one. He'd used the biscuits to lure Goliath into his garden. "I hope ye won't mind my borrowing your dog a wee while?"

asked Mr. MacGregor, a little
sheepishly.

"Not at all," said David politely.
"But why?"

Mr. MacGregor came closer to the fence. "I was reading the story in the paper—aboot the dog having a nose for buried treasure?"

David still looked puzzled.

Mr. MacGregor went on, "I was thinking he was awfu' keen on my flower bed. If he's going to find me some buried treasure—he can dig as many holes as he likes!"

About the author

After studying at Cambridge, Terrance Dicks became an advertising copy-writer, then a radio and television scriptwriter and script editor. His career as a children's author began with the *Dr Who* series and he has now written a variety of other books on subjects ranging from horror to detection.